MADAME BUTTERFLY

MADAME BUTTERFLY

John Luther Long

www.General-Books.net

Publication Data:

Title: Madame Butterfly
Author: John Luther Long
General Books publication date: 2009
Original publication date: 1903
Original Publisher: Century Co.
Subjects: Americans
Japan
Drama / American
Fiction / Classics
Fiction / Literary
History / Asia / Japan

CONTENTS

1

SECTION 1

dithyrambics. But they have detected and scorned it, and it is now returned with the reproach that eight pages are thus left by my default to be filled or something will happen to the book and to the public – and to me.

" Now be sensible," they say, or words to that flattering effect, " and tell the plain people plainly how the story was born; how it went out into the world and touched the great universal heart, as ready to be touched as some rare instrument and as difficult; how it became a play – grand opera (the very first American story any European composer has set to music, according to those who are wise in such matters – though 7 don't believe it); what the people have said about it, – et cetera."

Well, here it is! Since they will not have the insidious poem, they shall tell it themselves – and have both the blame and the praise. They printed it. The people read it, and said and wrote things about it – some good, some bad. But, happily, they who liked Cho- Cho-San were more than they who did not; and so she laughed and wept her way into some pretty hard hearts, and lived – not entirely in vain.

And then she went upon the stage and made Miss Bates and herself so famous that we had to write a bigger play for them. And they beckoned for her across the sea, where, in London, Signore Puccini saw her, and when she comes back she will be a song! Sad, sad indeed, but yet a song!

What the people have said to me about her has been almost entirely by way of question. And the most frequent of these has been whether I, too, was n't sorry for Cho. To this I answer, with confusion, Yes. When she wept I wanted to – *if I did rit;* and when she smiled I think I did; but when she laughed I know I did.

For, you will remember that at first she laughed oftener than she wept, and at last she wept oftener than she laughed – so one could n't help it.

And where has she gone? I do not know. I lost sight of her, as you did, that dark night she fled with Trouble and Suzuki from the little, empty, happy house on Higashi Hill, where she was to have had a honeymoon of nine hundred and ninety-nine years!

And is she a fancy, or does she live? Both.

And where is Pinkerton? At least not in the United States navy – if the savage letters I receive from his fellows are true.

Concerning the genesis of the story I know nothing. I think no one ever does. What process of the mind produces such things? What tumult of the emotions sets them going? I do not know. Perhaps it is the sum of one's fancies of life – not altogether sad, not altogether gay, a thing to be borne, often for others whom its leaving would mar. Perhaps the sleepless gods who keep the doors of life did not close them*quite*upon some other incarnation? For gods who never sleep may sometimes nod.

Finally, what matter? Here in this book is Cho-Cho-San, born again with all her little sins anew upon her head. And some of these the scribbler who here writes knows as well as they who, long since void of sentiment, sit in their chairs where words are made, and con them, and set them forth, forgetting that there may be something better had for good will and good searching. But there are sins one loves. So I love those of Cho. And I would have this Cho-Cho-San no more perfect than the world has cared to have her.

And this is she. Here is no "revised " edition. It has all the human, all the literary faults it had at first – and, may I hope, still its little charm?

So, Messieurs, Mesdames, I beg here, in your presence, that all the Gods of Luck will smile on this reincarnation!

Go-men nasai. Oitoma itashimasho.

J. L. L.

SCHLAFEWOHLPLATZ,

August 27, 1903.

2

SECTION 2

MADAME BUTTERFLY

Sayre'sPrescription

SAYRE had counseled him on the voyage out (for he had repined ceaselessly at what he called their banishment to the Asiatic station) to wait till they arrived.*He*had never regarded service in Japanese waters as banishment, he said, and he had been out twice before.

Pinkerton had just come from the Mediterranean.

" For lack of other amusement," continued Sayre, with a laugh, " you might get yourself married and – "

Pinkerton arrested him with a savage snort.

" You are usually merely frivolous, Sayre; but to-day you are silly."

Without manifest offense, Sayre went on:

" When I was out here in 1890 – "

"The story of the Pink Geisha?"

" Well – yes," admitted Sayre, patiently.

" Excuse me, then, till you are through." He turned to go below.

"Heard it, have you?"

" A thousand times – from you and others."

Sayre laughed good-naturedly at the gallant exaggeration, and passed Pinkerton his cigarette-case.

" Ah – ever heard who the man was?"

"No." He lighted his cigarette. " That has been your own little mystery – apparently."

"Apparently?"

" Yes; we all knew it was yourself."

" It was n't," said Sayre, steadily. " It was my brother." He looked

away.

"Oh!"

" He 's dead."

" Beg pardon. You never told us that."

" He went back; could n't find her."

" And you advise me also to become a subject for remorse? That's good of you."

" It is not quite the same thing. There is no danger of you losing yourhead for – " he glanced uncertainly at Pinkerton, then ended lamely – " any one. The danger would probably be entirely with – the other per

son."

" Thanks," laughed Pinkerton; " that 's more comforting."

" And yet," mused Sayre, " you are hard to comfort – humanly speak- ing."

Pinkerton smiled at this naive but quite exact characterization of himself.

" You are," continued Sayre, hesitating for the right word – " imper

vious."

" Exactly," laughed Pinkerton. " I *don't*see much danger to myself in your pre-scription. You have put itin rather an attractive light. The idea cannot be entirely disreputable if your brother Jack used it. We lower- class fellows used to call him Agamemnon, you remember."

" It is not my prescription," said Sayre, briefly, leaving the deck.

SECTION 3

II

MR. B. F. PIKKERTON AND HIS WAY

BUT Pinkerton not only got himself married; he provided himself with an establishment – creating his menage in quite his own way and entirely for his own comfort.

With the aid of a marriage-broker, he found both a wife and a house in which to keep her. This he leased for nine hundred and ninety-nine years. Not, he explained to his wife later, that he could hope for the felicity of residing there with her so long, but because, being a mere " barbarian," he could not make other legal terms. He did not mention that the lease was determinable, nevertheless, at the end of any month, by the mere neglect to pay the rent. Details were distasteful to Pinkerton; besides, she would probably not appreciate the humor of this.

Some clever Japanese artisans then made the paper walls of the pretty house eye-proof, and, with their own adaptations of American hardware, the openings cunningly lockable. The rest was Japanese.

Madame Butterfly laughed, and asked him why he had gone to all that trouble – in Japan!

" To keep out those who are out, and in those who are in," he replied, with an amorous threat in her direction.

She was greatly pleased with it all, though, and went about jingling her new keys and her new authority like toys, – she had only one small maid to command, – until she learned that among others to be excluded were her own relatives.

There had been what her husband called an appalling horde of these at the wedding (they had come with lanterns and banners and disturbing evidences of good will), and he asked her, when she questioned him, whether she did not think they would be a trifle wearisome.

"*You*thing so? " she asked in turn.

" Emphatically," said her husband.

She grew pale; she had not expected quite such an answer. A Japanese would have said no, but would have left an interrogation in one's mind.

He laughed consolingly.

" Well, Ane-San" (which meant only " elder sister": there are no terms of endearment in the Japanese language), "you will have to get along without ancestors. Think of the many people who would like to do that, and be comforted."

" Who? " She had never heard of such a thing.

" People, for instance, whose ancestors have perished on the gallows, or, in America, have practised trades."

She did not understand, as often she did not, and he went on:

" I shall have to serve in the capacity of ancestors, – let us say ances- tors-at-large, – and the real ones will have to go – or rather not come."

Again he had the joke to himself; his wife had gone away to cry.

At first she decided to run away from him. But this, she reflected, would not probably please her relatives, since they had unanimously agreed upon the marriage for her. Besides, she preferred to remain. She had acquired a strange liking for Pinkerton and her new way of life. Finally she undertook a weak remonstrance – a very strong one, in fact, for a Japanese wife; but Pinkerton encouraged her pretty domestic autonomy. Her airs of authority were charming. And they grew more and more so.

"Mr. B. F. Pikkerton," – it was this, among other things, he had taught her to call him, – " I lig if you permit my august ancestors visit me. I lig ver'*moach*if you*please*permit that unto me."

Her hair had been newly dressed for the occasion, and she had stuck a poppy in it. Besides, she put her hand on his arm (a brave thing for her to do), and smiled wistfully up at him. And when you know what Cho-Cho- San's smile was like, – and her hand – and its touch, – you will wonder how Pinkerton resisted her. However, he only laughed at her, – good- naturedly always, – and said no.

" We can't adopt a whole regiment of back numbers, you know. You are back number enough for me."

And though he kissed her, she went away and cried again; and Japanese girls do not often cry.

He could not understand how important this concession was to her. It must be confessed that he did not try to understand. Sayre, with a little partizanship, explained to him that in Japan filial affection is the paramount motive, and that these " ancestors," living and dead, were his wife's sole link to such eternal life as she hoped for. He trusted that Pin- kerton would not forget this.

He would provide her a new motive, then, Pinkerton said, – perhaps meaning himself, – and a new religion if she *must* have one – himself, again. So when she, at his motion, diffidently undertook to clothe the phantoms which made up her " religion," Pinkerton expounded what he called the easier Western plan of salvation – seriously, too, considering that all his communications to her were touched with whimsy. This was inevitable – to Pinkerton. After all, she *was* quite an impossible little thing, outside of lacquer and paint. But he struck deeper than he knew; for she went secretly to the church of the missionary who served on the opposite hill, and heard the same thing, and learned, moreover, that she might adopt this new religion at any time she chose – even the eleventh hour.

She went out joyously; not to adopt his religion, it is true, but to hold it in reserve if her relatives should remain obdurate. Pinkerton, to his relief, heard no more of it.

4

SECTION 4

III

A MOON-GODDESS TRULY

BUT his wife's family (the word has a more important application there than here) held a solemn conference, and, as the result of it, certain of them waited upon Lieutenant Pinkerton, and, with elaborate politeness, intimated that his course had theretofore been quite unknown in Japan. This was their oblique way of saying that it was unsatisfactory. They pointed out with patient gravity that he would thus limit his wife's opportunities of reappearing on earth in a higher form of life.

Pinkerton smilingly remarked that he was not sure that it would be best for his wife to reappear on earth in a higher form. She would probably accomplish mischief enough in this very charming one – as she was in fact doing.

" Do you know," he continued to the spokesman, " that you look exactly like a lacquered tragedy mask I have hanging over my desk? "

One must have seen one of these masks to appreciate this.

But they all laughed good-naturedly, as their host had designed, and quite forgot their errand. And Pinkerton labored that they should remember it no more. This was quite Japanese. In the politest way possible he made them drink his liquors and

ining on the mats

smoke his tobacco (in the generous Western fashion), either of which operations was certain to make a Japanese very ill. This was thoroughly like Pinkerton.

They protested a deal of friendship for Pinkerton that night; but at the final conference, where Cho- Cho-San was solemnly disowned, none were more gloomily unfriendly than they who had eaten and drunken with him.

" I did the very best I could for you, little moon-goddess," said Pinkerton to his wife; "but they were proof against my best wine and tobacco."

She bent her head in reflection a moment.

" Ah, you mean – I begin learnyou, Mr. B. F. Pikkerton! You mean they*not*proof. Aha! "

And Pinkerton delightedly embraced her.

" You are no longer a back number," he said.

" Aha! Tha' 's what / thing. Now I bed you I know what*is*that bag nomber!"

"Well?"

" People lig I*was.*"

"Exactly."

" But not people lig I*am? *"

"No; you are up-to-date."

" I egspeg I ought be sawry? " She sighed hypocritically.

"Exactly why, my moon-maid?"

" Account they outcasting me. Aeverybody thing me mos' bes'wicked in all Japan. Nobody speak to me no more – they all outcast me*aexcep*'jus' you; tha' 's why I ought be sawry."

She burst into a reckless laugh, and threw herself like a child upon him.

" But tha' 's ezag' why I am*not!*Wha"s use lie? It is not inside me – that sawry. Me? I 'm mos' bes' happy female woman in Japan – mebby in that whole worl'. What you thing? "

He said honestly that he thought she was, and he took honest credit for it.

5

SECTION 5

IV

TROUBLE MEANING JOY

AND after his going, in the whim-*l*.sical delight they had practised together, she
named the baby, when it came, Trouble. Every Japanese baby begins with a temporary
name; it may be anything, almost, for the little time. She was quite sure he would
like the way she had named him Trouble – meaning joy. That was his own oblique
way. As for his permanent name, – he might have several others before, – that was
for him to choose when he returned. And this event was to happen, according to his
own words, when the robins nested again.

And spring and the robins had come.

Allthis to explain why Madame Butterfly and her baby were reclining on the
immaculate mats in attitudes of artistic abandon, instead of keeping an august state, as
all other Japanese mothers and babes were at this moment doing. American women,
we are told, assume more fearless attitudes in the security of their boudoirs than
elsewhere. Japanese women, never. Their conduct is eternally the same. It must be
as if some one were looking on – always. There is no privacy for them short of the
grave. They have no secure boudoirs.

But Madame Butterfly (throughthe courtesy of her American husband) had both these. It will therefore be argued, perhaps, that she is not a typical Japanese woman. But it is only Lieutenant Pinkerton's views about which we are presently concerned. He called her an American refinement of a Japanese product, an American improvement in a Japanese invention, and so on. And since he knew her best, his words concerning her should have a certain ex-cathedra authority. I know no more.

Andshe and the maid, and the baby too, were discussing precisely the matters which have interested us hitherto – Pinkerton, his baby, his imminent return, etc.

Cho-Cho-San, with a deft jerk that was also a caress, brought the baby into her lap as she sat suddenly up.

" Ah,*you* – you think he is just like any other baby. But – he is a miracle! Yes! " she insisted belligerently. " The Sun-Goddess sent him straight from the Bridge of Heaven! Because of those prayers so early – oh, so*very*early – in the morning. Oh, that is the time to pray!" She turned the baby violently so that she might see his eyes. " Now did any one*ever*hear of a Japanese baby with purple eyes?"

She held him over against the dwarfed wistaria which grew in a flat bronze koro at the tokonoma, full of purple blossoms. She addressed the maid Suzuki, who stood by, happy
as herself, apparently aware that this subject must always be discussed vehemently.

"As purple as that! Answer me, thou giggler; is it not so? Speak! I*will*have an answer! "

Then the maid laughed out a joyous no. If she cherished the Eastern reservations concerning blue eyes and pink cheeks, it was a less heinous offense to lie about it a little than to assert it impolitely. Besides, neither she nor any one else could resist the spirits of her pretty mistress. And these spirits had grown joyously riotous since her marriage and its unfettering.

" Nor yet so bald of his head? Say so! Quickly! " she insisted, with the
"<But – he is a miracle! Yes!"
manner of Pinkerton – such is example!

The maid also agreed to this.

And then Cho-Cho-San flung the kicking youngster high above her, turned abandonedly over on her back (in charming, if forbidden, postures), and juggled with him there.

" But ah! you*will*have hair, will you not? – as long and glittering as that of the American women. I will not endure thee else." She became speciously savage. " Speak, thou beggar, speak!"

" Goo-goo," said the baby, endeavoring diligently to obey.

She shook him threateningly.

" Ah-h-h! You making that non-*senze*with your parent? Now what*is*that you speaking with me? Jap'- nese? If it is, I – " She threatened him direly. But he had evidently already learned to understand her; he gurgled again. " Listen!*No*one shall speak anything but United States' languages in these house!*Now!*What you thing? You go'n' go right outside shoji firs' thing you do that!" She resumed her own English more ostentatiously, – she forgot it herself sometimes, – and pretended to pitch the baby through the fragile paper wall.

" Also, tha' 's one thing*aeverybody*got recomleck – account it is his house, his wife, his bebby, his maiden, his moaney – oh, – *aeveryth'mg*is hisj An* he say, those time he go'n' 'way, that aearcep' we all talking those United States' languages when he come, he go'n' bounce us all.*Well!*I don' git myself bounce, Mr. Trouble! An' you got loog out you don', aha! Sa-ay, me? I thing if we doing all those thing he as' us, he go'n' take us at those United States America, an' live in his castle. Then he never*kin*bounce us, aha!" A SONG OF SORROW – AND DEATH

AND HEAVEN

A BIRD flew to the vine in the little porch.

"Ah, Suzuki!"

But the maid had withdrawn. She clapped her hands violently for her to return.

" Now why*do*you go away when " – her momentary anger fled, and she laughed – " when birds flying to the wistaria? Go quickly, little maiden, and see if he is a robin, and if he has completed his nest – quickly."

The maid returned, and said that he was indeed a robin, but that he had no nest there as yet.

" Oh,*how*he is slow! Suzuki, let us fine 'nother robin, one that is more industri-ous – an' domes-tic, aha, ha, ha!"

" They are all alike," said the girl, cynically.

"They – *not!*Say so!"

Suzuki giggled affirmatively. When her mistress took so violently to English she preferred to express herself in this truly Japanese fashion.

" Inform me, if you please, how much nearer beggary we are to-day than yesterday, Suzuki."

The girl had exact information for her on this subject. She said they had*jus*t seventeen yen, fifty-four sen, two rin.

" Alas – alas!*How*we have waste his beau-tiful moaneys! Tha' 's shame.*But*he will not permit that we starve – account he know we have no one*aexcep'*him. We all outcasted. Now loog*how*that is bad!*So*jus' when it is all gone he will come with more – lig the stories of ole Kazabu.*Oh!*lig story of Uncombed Ronin, who make a large oath that he go'n' be huge foo-1 if he dress his hair until his lord arrive back from the banishment.*Lo!*when they cutting his hade off him, account he don' comb his hair, his lord arrive back, an' say, 'What they doing with him?' – an' reward him great deal, account he constant*un*til he 'mos' dead.*So,*jus' when we go'n' out on the street, – mebby to fine him, – you with Trouble on your back, me with my samisen, standing up bi- fore all the people, singing funeral songs, with faces, oh, 'bout 'mos' so long," – she illustrated liberally, – " sad garments, hair all ruffled – so, dancing liddle – so," – she indicated how she should dance, – " an' saying out ver' loud, ' O ye people! Listen, for the loave of all the eight hundred thou- san' gods and goddesses! Behole, we, a poor widow, an' a bebby what got purple eyes, which had one hosban', which gone off at United States America, to naever return no more – *naever! Aexcep'*you have seen him? No? See! This what I thing. Oh, how that is mos' tarrible! We giving up all our august ancestors, an' gods, an' people, an' country, – oh,*aevery*-thing, – jus' for him, an' now he don' naever come no more! Oh,*how*that is sad! Is it not? Also, he don'even divorce us, so that we kin marry with 'nother mans an' git some food.*He?*He don' even*thing*'bout it! Not lid- die bit! He forgitting us – alas!*But*we got keep his house nine hundred an' ninety-nine year! Now thing 'bout*that!*An' we go'n' starve bi- fore, a&arcep' you giving us – ah-ah-*ah!*jus' one sen! two sen! mebby fi' sen! Oh, for the loave of sorrow, for the loave of constancy, for the loave of death, jus' – one – sen! Will you please pity us? In the name of themerciful Kwannon we beg. Loog! To move your hearts in the inside you, we go'n' sing you a song of – sorrow – an' death – an' heaven."

She had acted it all with superb spirit, and now she snatched up her samisen, and dramatized this also; and so sure was she of life and happiness that this is the song of sorrow and death she sang:

" Hikari nodokeki haru no nobe,

Niwo sakura-nohana sakari,

Mure kuru hito no tanoshiki ni,

Shibashi uki yo ya wasururan.

" Sunshine on a quiet plain in spring,

The perfume of the blooming cherry-

blossoms,

The joy of the gathering crowd,

Filled with love, forget the care of life."

And then, as always, abandonment and laughter.

" Aha, ha, ha! Aha, ha, ha! What you thing, liddle maiden? Tha' 's good song 'bout sorrow, an' death, f

an' heaven? Aha, ha, ha! What – you – thing? Speak! Say so!"

She tossed the samisen to its place, and sprang savagely at the maid.

" If that Mr. B. F. Pikkerton see us doing alig those – " ventured the maid, in the humor of her mistress.'

"O-o-o! You see his eye flame an' scorch lig lightening! O-o-o! He snatch us away to the house – so – so – *so!*"

The baby was the unfortunate subject for the illustration of this. He began to whimper.

She field him over against the dwarfed wistaria

" Rog-a-by, bebby, off in Japan,

You jus' a picture off of a fan."

This was from Pinkerton. She had been the baby then.

" Ah, liddle beggar, he di'n' know he go'n' make those poetries for you! He don' suspect of you whichever.*W ell I*I bed you we go'n' have some fun when he*do.*Oh, Suzuki! Some day, when the emperor go abroad, we will show him. You got say these way" – she changed her voice to what she fancied an impressive male basso: "'Behole, Heaven-Descended- Ruler- Everlasting- Great- Japan, the first of your subjecks taken his eye out those ver' blue heaven whence you are descend!' Hence the emperor loog on him; then he*stop*an' loog; he kin naever git enough loogs. Then he make Trouble a large prince! An' me? He jus' say onto me: ' Continue that you bring out such sons.' Aha, ha, ha! What you thing?"

The maid was frankly skeptical.

" At least you kin do lig the old nakodo wish you – for you are most beautiful."

Cho-Cho-San dropped the baby with a reckless thud, and sprang at her again. She gripped her throat viciously, then flung her, laughing, aside.

" Speak concerning marriage once more, an' you die. An' tha' 's 'nother thing. You got know at his United States America, if one is marry one got stay marry – oh, for aever an'aever!*Yaes!*Nob'y cannot git himself divorce,*aexc&p*'in a large courthouse an' jail. Tha' 's way with he – that Mr. B. F. Pikkerton – an' me – that Mrs. B. F. Pikkerton. If he aever go'n' divorce me, he got take me at those large jail at that United States America. Tha' 's lot of trouble; hence he rather stay marry with me. Also, he*lig*be marry with me. Now loog! He leave me a 'mos' largest lot money in Japan; he give me his house for live inside for nine hundred an' ninety-nine year. I cannot go home at my grandmother, account he make them outcast me. Sa-ay, you liddle foolish! He coming when the robins nest again. Aha! What you thing? Say so! "

The maid should have been excused for not being always as recklessly jubilant as her mistress; but she never was. And now, when she chose silence rather than speech (which was both more prudent and more polite), she took it very ill.

6

SECTION 6

VI

DIVINE FOOLERY

IF Pinkerton had told her to go home, even though she had no home to go to, she would have been divorced without more ado. Perhaps she was logical (for she reasoned as he had taught her – she had never reasoned before) in considering that as he had distinctly told her not to do so, it was an additional surety for his return.

Cho-Cho-San again took up the happier side of the matter. The baby was asleep.

" An' also, what you thing we bed- der doing when he come? "

She was less forcible now, because less certain. This required planning to get the utmost felicity out of it – what she always strovfe for.

"Me? – I thing I – *dunno, "*the maid confessed diplomatically.

"Aha, ha, ha! You dunnof Of course you dunno whichever! Well – I go'n' tell you." The plan had been born and matured that instant in her active little brain. "Jus' recom- leck 't is a secret among you an' me. We don' tell that Mr. Trouble. Hoash! He don' kin keep no secret.*Well,*listen! We go'n' watch with that spying-glass till his ship git in. Then we go'n' put cherry-blossomsaeverywhere; an' if 't is night, we go'n' hang up 'bout' 'mos' one thou- san' lanterns – 'bout 'mos' one thou- san'! Then we – *wait.*Jus' when we see him coming up that hill – so – so – so – *so, "* – she lifted her kimono, and strode masculinely about the apartment, – " then! We hide behine the shoji, where there are holes to peep." She glanced about to find them. " Alas! they all mended shut!*But"* – she savagely ran her finger through the paper – " we soon make some, aha, ha, ha! So!" She made another for the maid. They illustrated this phase of her mood with their eyes at the holes. " Then we lie quiet lig mice, an' make believe we gone 'way. Better n't we leave liddlenote: ' Gone 'way foraever. Sayonara, Butterfly'? No; tha' 's too long for him. He git angery those ways on the first word, an' say those remark 'bout debbil, an' hell, an' all kind loud languages. Tha' 's time, bifore he gitting*too*angery, to rush out, an' jump all roun' his neck, aha! " This was also illustrated.

But, alas! the maid was too realistic.

" Sa-oy.' not*you* – jump roun' his neck? – jus'*me."*

Cho-Cho-San paused ecstatically. But the maid would not have it so. She had seen them practise such divine foolery, – very like too reckless children, – but never had she seen anything with such dramatic promise as this.

"Oh! an' what he say*then,"*she begged, with wild interest, " an' what he*dot"*

Madame Butterfly was reenergized by the maid's applause.

" Ah-h-h! " she sighed. " He don'*say* – jus' he*kiss*us, oh, 'bout three – seven – ten – a thousan' time! An' amberace us two thousan' time 'bout 'mos' – tha' 's what he*do* – till we got make him stop, aha, ha, ha! account he might – might – *kill*us! Tha' 's*ver*'bad – to be kill kissing."

Her extravagant mood infected the maid. She had long ago begun to wonder whether, after all, this American passion of affection was altogether despicable. She remembered that her mistress had begun by regarding it thus; yet now she was the most daringly happy woman in Japan.

" Say more," the maid pleaded.

Cho-Cho-San had a fine fancy, and the nesting of the robins could not, at the longest, be much longer delayed now; she let it riot.

" Well," – she was making it up as she went, – " when tha' 's all done, he loog roun' those ways lig he doing 'mos' always, an' he see sump'n', an' he say: 'Oh, '*d-lo* – '*el-lo*Where you got that chile? ' I say: ' Ah – oh – *ah!*I thing mebby you lig own one, an' I buy 'm of a man what di'n' wan' no bebby with those purple eye an' bald hairs.' And he as' me, ' What you pay?' Americans always as' what you pay. I say: ' Oh, lenime see. I

Juggled with him

thing, two yen an' two sen. Tha' 's too moach for bald bebby?' What you thing? But tha' 's a time he saying: ' I bed you tha' 's a liar; an' you fooling among me.' Then he gitting angery, an' I hurry an' say, one las' time, ' Tha' 's right. I tole you liddle lie for a*fun.*I di'n' pay nawthing for him,*aexcep' – sa.-ay! –* ' Then I whisper a thing inside his ear, – jus' a liddle thing, – an' he*see!*Aha, ha, ha! Then he say once more, las' time, – ah, what you thing, Suzuki?"

But the girl would not diminish her pleasure by guessing.

"'Godamighty!' Aha, ha, ha!" "Tha' 's all things you know?" questioned the maid, reproachfully, " an' all things you do? "

She had a right to feel that she had been defrauded out of a proper denouement.

"Ah-h-h-h! What would you have that is more? Jus' joy an' glory for- aevermore! Tha' 's 'nough. What you thing? You know that song?

" T is life when we meet,

'T is death when we part."

Her mistress had grown plaintive in those two lines.

" I hear him sing that," murmured the maid, comfortingly.

Her spirits vaulted up again.

" But ah! You aever hear him sing – ? "

She snatched up the samisen again, and to its accompaniment sang, in the pretty jargon he had taught her (making it as grotesque as possible, the more to amuse him):

" I call her the belle of Japan – of Japan; Her name it is O Cho-Cho-San – Cho-Cho-San; Such tenderness lies in her soft almond

eyes, I tell you she 's just ichi ban."

" Tha' 's *me* – aha, ha, ha! Sa-oy – you thing he aever going away again when he got that liddle chile, an' the samisen, an' the songs, an' all the joy, an' – an' *me?* "And another richly joyous laugh.

" Oh, you an' the samisen an' joy – poof!" said the maid. "But the chile – tha' 's 'nother kind thing. *A* excep' *he* grow up, an' go 'way after his father?"

She was odiously unsatisfied. She would leave nothing to fate – to heaven – Shaka. But out of her joyous future her mistress satisfied even this grisly doubt.

" Ah-h-h! *But* we go'n' have *more* lig steps of a ladder, up, up, up! An' all purple eyes – oh, aevery one! An' all males! Then, if one go 'way, we got 'nother an' 'nother an' 'nother. Then, how *kin* he, that Mr. B. F. Pik- kerton, aever go 'way? Aha!"

" Yaet, O Cho-Cho-San, if you – "

Was this a new doubt? It will never be known.

" Stop! Tha' 's 'nother thing. You got call me O Cho-Cho-San, *an'* 'Missus Ben-ja-meen Frang-a-leen Pikkerton. Sa-oy; you notize how that soun' gran' when my hosban' speaking it that aways? Yaes! 'Mos' lig I was a' emperess. Listen! I tell you 'nother thing, which is 'nother secret among you an' me jus': I thing it is more nize to be call that away – jus' Missus Ben-ja-meen Frang-a- leen Pikkerton – than Heaven-Descended-Female- Ruler- Everlasting- Great-Japan, aha! Sa-oy; how I loog if I a' emperess? What you thing? "

She imitated the pose and expression of her empress very well.

" If your face liddle longer you loog ezag' lig," said the maid.

But her mistress was inclined to be more modest.

" Ah, no. *But* I tell you who loog lig a' emperor – jus' ezag' – that Mr. B. F. Pikkerton, when he got that unicorn upon him, with gole all up in front an' down behine! "

And at this gentle treason there was no protest from the patriotic maid.

7

SECTION 7

VII

HOW HE DIDN'tUNDERSTAND HER WHICHEVER

baby continued to sleep. He-L rather justified the praises of his mother. He was as good as a Japanese baby, and as good-looking as an American one.

Somebody was without. There was a polite and subdued clattering of clogs in the entrance.

" Gomen nasai " ("I beg your pardon").

It was a familiar, deprecatory voice, accompanied by the clapping of hands.

Cho-Cho-San smiled wearily, and called the maid.

" Oh, Suzuki, Goro the nakodo – he is without. Shaka and all the gods defend us now!"

The two exchanged glances of amusement, and the maid proceeded to admit him.

Madame Butterfly received him with the odious lack of ceremony her independent life with Pinkerton had bred. She was imperially indifferent. The go-between pointed out how sad this was to as beautiful a woman as she.

" Is it a trouble to you? " she asked, perking her head aside.

The nakodo only sighed gloomily.

Madame Butterfly laughed.

" Poor, nize liddle old man," said *"Ah, Suzuki!"*
she, with specious pity, in politest English; " do not trouble 'bout me. Do not arrive any more if it pains you."

" I must; you have no parents now – nor any one. You are outcast."

" Ah-h-h! *But* will you not permit *me* to suffer the lack? "

" But you will never be married!"

"Again?"

"Well – yes, again, then."

"How *tarrible!*"

He took this quite seriously, and became more cheerful.

" Yes; a beautiful woman like you must have a husband."

"Yaes. Thangs; I got *one.* Do you perhaps mean more? "

" I mean a Japanese husband."

" Oh – ah? That will have me a *month,* and then divorce me? And then another, and another, and another?"

She was becoming belligerent.

" How is it better with you now? "

She recovered her good humor.

" At America one is married for- a *ever* – a *excep* 'the other die. Aha! What you thing? Your marriages are not so."

She had been speaking indifferently both languages, and now the nakodo, who was not apt at English, begged her to explain this in Japanese. She did so.

" Yamadori has lived long at America, and he says it is not thus. Is it not safe to rely upon his excellent wisdom?"

" No; for I, which am foolish, are wiser than both you an' he. */* know. You jus' guess. A *everybody* got stay marry at United States America. No one can git divorce, a *excep* 'he stay in a large court-house, all full judges with long faces, an' bald on their heads, long, long time; mebby two – four – seven year! Now jus' thing 'bout that – *how* that is tiresome! Tha' 's why no one don' git no divorce; they too tire' to wait. Firs', the man he got go an' stan' bifore those judge, an' tell all he thing 'bout it. Then the woman she got. Then some lawyers quarrel with those judge; an' then the judges git jury, an' as' 'em what they thing 'bout it; an' if they don' know they *all* git put in jail till they git done *thinging* 'bout it, an' whether they go'n' git divorce or not. Aha! "

" Where did you learn that? " asked the old nakodo, aghast.

"Oh – ah – that Mr. B. F. Pikker- ton" – she assumed a grander air – " that Mr. Ben-ja-meen Frang-a- leen Pikkerton – my hosban' – " She smiled engagingly, and held out her pretty hands, as who should say: " Is not *that* sufficient? "

It was so evidently the invention of Pinkerton that it seemed superfluous to make the explanation. The nakodo said curtly that he did not believe it.

Not believe what Mr. B. F. Pinker- ton had said!

Cho-Cho-San was exasperated. The engaging smile had been wasted. She *flung* the blue-eyed baby up before him.

" Well, then, do you believe *that? "*

She laughed almost malignantly. The marriage-broker gulped down this fearful indignity as best he might. He hoped there were not going to be any more such women in Japan as the result of foreign marriages. Still, even this phase of the situation had been discussed with his client.

" But Yamadori, who was bred to the law, tells me that our law prevails in such a matter, the marriage having taken place here."

She gave a gasp, and cried like a savage wounded animal:

"Yamadori – lies!"

The nakodo was silenced. Shecrushed the baby so fiercely to her breast that he began to cry.

*"Sh!"*she commanded harshly. He looked up for an incredulous instant, then burrowed his head affright- edly into her kimono. She turned upon the nakodo in magnificent scorn.

" Oh – *you – foo-el!*You thing he naever arrive back. Tha' 's what you thing – in secret! He? He*do!"*

She snatched a photograph from an easel at the tokonoma, tore the child from his hiding, and held them up together. Her purpose was quite evident.

The nakodo was thoroughly frightened. She recovered her poise – and her control of the situation.

*"Now*what you thing? Aha, ha, ha! Sa-ay – I bed you all moaneys he go'n' come 'mos' one millions mile for see that chile! Tha' 's what I all times praying Shaka an' the august- nesses for – one chile ezag' lig him.*Well, sa-ay!*I got him. An' now that Mr. Ben-ja-meen Frang-a-leen Pik- kerton he*got*come back – hoarry – even if he don' lig. He cannot stand it. But he do lig."

All her passion was gone now, and her sure gladness returned. She was naive and intimate and confidential again.

" Sa-oy/ Firs' I pray his large American God, – that huge God- amighty, – but tha' 's no use. He don' know me where I live. Then I pray Shaka an' all the kaimyo of the augustnesses in the god-house. I thing they don' hear me, account they outcasted me when I marry with that Mr. B. F. Pikkerton.*But"* – she smiled at her pretty celestial cajolery – " I pray them so long an' so moach more than they aever been pray with bifore that they feel good all times, an' – an' " " – there was finality in this – " an'*'t is*use. An' mebby I not*all*outcasted! Don' tell him. He – he laugh upon my gods, an' say they jus' wood an' got no works in them. An' he all times call the augustnesses bag nombers! Jus' he don' know till he fine out. Aha, ha, ha!"

" If he returns he will probably take the child away with him – that is his right," chanted the sad-faced nakodo.

But nothing could ruffle MadameButterfly now. She laughed sibilantly at this owl-like ignorance.

" Oh-h-h!*How*you don' know things!*How*you don' onderstan' me what I mean, whichever! Of course he take that chile away with him – of course! An'*me* – me also; an' Suzuki, aha! An' we go an' live in his castle for aever an' aever! "

The improbability of changing the girl's point of view began to dawn upon the slow intellect of the nakodo.

" At least, Yamadori wishes for a look-at meeting. I have promised him. Will you not grant this? "

Cho-Cho-San shook her head at him knowingly.

" An' if I do not, he not go'n' pay you one present? "

She laughed wildly, and the nakodo by a grin admitted the impeachment.

" Well," – the spirit of mischief possessed the girl, – "*sa-ay* – I don' keer. Let him come. He lig for see me; I lig for see him. An' if I say I go'n' marry him, he got hoarry an' marry me right away. Aha! What you thing 'bout*those?* "

The nakodo said delightedly that that was precisely what he sought.

" Yaes;*but*suppose they put me in a large jail, an' got loog out between bar – so," – she illustrated, – "an' don' git nawthing for eat; he go'n' stay all times behine my side, an' comforting me? Hoi' my hand? Lemme weep upon him? I dunno. Mebby they cut my hade off me. Then he got git his

The nakodo fixed that day a u<eek

hade cut off, too, an' go the road to Meido together – with – without those hade! Oh,*how*that is tarrible! An' suppose" – she whispered it horridly – " that Mr. B. F. Pikkerton – aha, ha, ha! – *arrive?* "

The nakodo was not sure how much of this was meant seriously. They were extremely unusual humors to him. But she had consented to the meeting, and he promptly took her at her word.

" When, then, will it please you to have me bring Yamadori? "

" When you lig – nize liddle ole friend."

The nakodo fixed that day a week.

As he was going, Cho-Cho-San laughingly asked:

" Sa-oy/ How often he been marry? "

" But twice," the nakodo replied virtuously.

"An' both times divorce?"

He admitted that this was the case.

" An' both times jus' on visit from United States America – jus'*liddle*visit? – so long?" She spread her hands.

Under her laughing gaze it seemed best to admit it.

" Oh!*he* – he jus' marry 'nother for fun – whenever he thing 'bout it. Then he forgit it when he don' thing 'bout it, and marry 'nother. Say so! "

He heard her laugh again as he left the courtyard; but he had confidence in the ability of Yamadori to accomplish his purpose if he could be brought into contact with her. He was one of the modern pensioned princes of Japan, a desirable matrimonial article, and preternaturally fascinating.

8

SECTION 8

VIII

THE BRIGHT RED SPOT IN CHO's
CHEEKS

THE look-at meeting came about as planned. There was a distinct air of state about Madame Butterfly's house on that day. The baby, and all the frivolities that attended him, were in banishment. The apartment had been enlarged by the rearrangement of the shoji. At the head of it, statuesque in her most brilliant attire, sat Cho-Cho-San. Japanese women are accomplished actresses; and looking in upon Cho-Cho-San just at the moment of Yamadori's arrival, one would not have known her. She was as unsmiling, as emotionless, as the Dai-Butsu.

The grave ceremonies attending the advent of a candidate for matrimony went forward with almost no recognition from Cho-Cho-San until they had come to the point where they might seat themselves before her, to inspect and be inspected. Then she struck her fan against her palm, and Suzuki appeared, and set the tobaco- bon between them.

Yamadori suggested somewhat the ready-made clothier – inevitable evidence of his transformation; otherwise he was the average modern Japanese, with high-gibbeted trousers, high collar, high hat, and eye-glass. He might not converse directly with

Cho-Cho-San, especially concerning the business in hand; but he was not prohibited from conferring with the nakodo about it in her presence. The rule of decorum for such an occasion simply decreed that she should be blind and deaf concerning what went on. The convenience of the arrangement is obvious. The nakodo, the representative of both parties, was happily permitted, on the part of the one, to regard what was happening as if it had not happened, and, on the part of the other, as if it had.

" She is quite as beautiful as you said," remarked Yamadori, after a careful inspection with his glass. The nakodo nodded virtuously, and filled his pipe. His client lighted a cigarette.

Cho-Cho-San did not even smile.

" And her father, you say, was on the emperor's side in the Satsuma rebellion?"

The marriage-broker satisfied his client to the last particular of her father's bloody sacrificial end at Jokoji.

" And you have told her faithfully of *me?* "He pausecl on the last word to note its effect upon Cho-Cho-San. There was none, and he hastened to add cumulatively, " And my august family?" He paused again. But again there was no sign from the lady of the house. She was staring out over his head. " And have offered her my miserable presents? "

To each of these the broker answered lugubriously yes.

" Then why, in the name of the gods, does she wait?"

The nakodo explained with a sigh that she had declined his presents.

" I will send her others. They shall be a thousand times more valuable. Since I have seen her I know that the first must have been an affront."

She kept her eyes up, but Yamadori unquestionably smiled in the direction of Cho-Cho-San – as if she were a woman of joy!

The light of battle came into the stony eyes of the girl. She clapped her hands almost viciously. The little maid appeared.

"Tea!" she said.

The maid brought the tea; and with that splendid light of danger still in her eyes, Cho-Cho-San served it. With the air of a princess she put on in an instant all the charms of a mous- mee. She gave back smile for smile now, and jest for jest. She begged Yamadori, with the most charming upward inflections, to put away his cigarette and take her shippo pipe, and he did it. *That* was Japanese, she said, her cigarettes were not. Was it not so? – with a resistless movement toward him. She let him touch her hands in the passage of the cups. She enveloped him with the perfume of her garments. She possessed him wholly in one dizzy instant.

" I will give her a castle to live in," said Yamadori, breathlessly.

The nakodo sighed. Cho-Cho-San refilled his pipe with an incomparable grace.

" Ah!" she permitted her lips to breathe – very softly.

" She shall have a thousand servants."

There was no audible response from the nakodo, but his eyes gleamed avidly.

Cho-Cho-San returned the pipe, smiling dazzlingly. It seemed almost yes with her.

" Everything her heart can wish! " cried Yamadori, recklessly.

The nakodo turned beseechingly toward the girl. She lifted her eyebrows. He did not understand. As she passed him she laughed.

"Is it enough?"

Still he did not understand.

" Have we earned the present? " she whispered.

" I will give a solemn writing," added Yamadori, fervidly.

" She still fancies herself perhaps married to the American," sighed the nakodo.

Yamadori laughed disagreeably.

" If your Excellency would condescend to explain – "

" Oh, she is not serious. A sailor has a sweetheart in every port, you know."

Cho-Cho-San whispered something to the nakodo. She still smiled.

" But she is perhaps his *wife,* "answered he, obediently.

" Yes," said Yamadori, as if they were the same.

Cho-Cho-San whispered again.

" But the child – there is a most accomplished child?" said the nakodo.

" Yes," said the traveled Japanese, with the same smile and the same intonation.

There was a distinct silence. Cho- Cho-San smiled more vividly. But her nostrils moved rapidly in and out. The nakodo grew anxious. Yamadori cast his eyes toward the ceiling, and continued:

" A sailor does not know the difference. In no other country are children esteemed as they are here. InAmerica it is different. People sometimes deny them. They are left in a basket at some other person's door. But the person does not receive them. They are then cared for by the municipality as waifs. It is shameful to be such a child. There are great houses and many officers in each city for the care of these. They are an odious class by themselves, and can never rise above their first condition."

The nakodo glanced askance at his client. He had not the slightest objection to a man who would lie a little to win his cause, but to lie too much was to lose it.

" I myself knew a man whose child became a cripple. He sent him to the mayor of the city, saying that as the cars of the city had injured him, the city must bring him up. He was sent to the poorhouse, and afterward to the stone-quarries. It was a most piteous sight."

Cho-Cho-San bent again to the ear of the old man. There was a tremor in her voice now.

" Had he eyes of purple? " asked the nakodo.

" He was beautiful of face; but surely eyes of purple are not desirable?" Yamadori brought his own down from the ceiling and leveled them at Cho-Cho-San. She still smiled, but there was a bright-red spot in each cheek now. " But he was misshapen, and he was never known to laugh. I saw many such. I saw a child whose father had deserted it, and the mother – "

Madame Butterfly clapped her hands again. The maid appeared promptly; she had expected the summons.

" Suzuki – good Suzuki, the excellent gentlemen – the august " – she swept a royal gesture toward them – " who have done us the honor to call, they wish to go hurriedly. Their shoes – will you not hasten them? "

With a final brilliant smile she turned her back upon them and left the room.

"Yourstory of the rejected child did it," reproached the nakodo, on the way.

" I had not got to the worst," said his client, ruefully. " I meant to cite an example exactly to suit her own case."

" Lucky she turned us out when she did, then."

"What do you mean, sir?" demanded the suitor, in sudden wrath.

" Oh," said the broker, in polite haste, " I was beginning to feel – ill."

The irony of this escaped the client. Still, Goro would have had a less opinion of Yamadori if, having lied once, he had not lied again in defense of the first.

Though Yamadori came no more, he had brought the serpent to Madame Butterfly's Eden.

9

SECTION 9

IX

"'boutBirds"

ONE day she took her courage, and the maid's too, for that matter, in both hands, and called upon the American consul. She saw the vice-consul. There was a west wind, and it was warm at Nagasaki. He was dozing. When he woke, Madame Butterfly was bowing before him. At a little distance was the maid with the blond baby strapped to her back. He was unable to account for them immediately.

" Goon night," said Cho-Cho-San, smiling amiably.

The consul glanced apprehensively about.

"Night! Not night, is it?"

They both discovered the error at the same instant.

" Ah! no, no, no! Tha' 's ww-take. Me – I 'm liddle raddle'. Aexcuse us. Tha' 's not nize, male'*mis-take.*We got call you good morning, I egspeg, or how do? What you thing?"

"Whichever you like," he answered, without a smile.

Then Cho-Cho-San waited for something further from the consul. Nothing came. She began to suspect that it was her business to proceed instead of his.

" I – I thing mebby you don' knowme? " she questioned, to give him a chance.

" Oh, yes, I do," declared the consul. In fact, everybody knew her, for one reason and another – her baby, her disowning, her beauty, her " American " marriage. " You are O Cho- Cho-San, the daughter – " he forgot her father's name, though he had often heard it. " You used to dance, did you not? "

"Aha! See! Tha' 's what I thing. You don' know me whichaever. I nobody's daughter; jus' Missus Ben- ja – no! Missus Frang-a-leen Ben-ja- meen – no, no,*no!*Missus Ben-ja- meen Frang-a-leen Pikkerton. Aev- erybody else outcast me. Aha, ha, ha! I liddle more raddle'."

" Oh! " The consul was genuinely surprised, and for the first time looked with interest at the child. Cho-Cho- San, to aid him, took Trouble from the maid. Finally he politely asked her what he could do for her.

" I got as' you a thing."

She returned the baby to the maid.

" Proceed," said the consul.

" You know 'bout birds in your country? "

"Yes, something."

"Ah! tha' 's what I thing. You know everything. Tha' 's why your country sen' you here – account you
ver' wise."

" You do me too much honor,' laughed the consul. "You – *don'* – know?"

It was tragically sudden

She was distinctly alarmed.

" Everything? No; only a few things."

*" But*you know 'bout birds – robins – jus' liddle robins? "

Her inflections denounced it a crime not to know. He was not proof against this, or against these.

" Oh, yes," he said; " of course."

"Aha! Of course. Tha' 's what I all times thinging. Tha' 's*mis-take*by you? "

They could laugh together now.

" Ah! Tell me, then, if you please, when do those robin nest again?*Me?*I thing it is later than in Japan, is it not? Account – jus'account the robin nesting again jus'*now*in Japan."

The consul said yes because the girlso evidently desired it – not because he knew.

"Aha! Tha' 's what I thing. Later – moach later than in Japan, is it not?"

Again her fervid emphasis obliged him to say yes, somewhat against his conscience.

" An' – *sa-ay!*When somebody git- ting marry with 'nother body at your America, don' he got stay marry?"

" Usually – yes; decidedly yes; even sometimes when he does n't wish to."

" An' don' madder where they live? "

" Not at all."

"Ah-h-h!*How*that is nize! Sa-oy; you know all 'bout*that.*What you thing? "

" Well, I know more about that than about ornithology. You see, I 've been married, but I 've never been a – a robin."

The joke passed quite unnoticed. She put her great question:

" An' no one can't git divorce from 'nother*aexcep*'in a large court-house full judge?"

" Yes," laughed the consul; " that is true."

" An' that take a ver' long time? "

" Yes; nearly always. The law's delay – "

" An' sometimes they git inside a jail?"

She was so avid that she risked the very great discourtesy of an interruption – and that, too, without a word of apology. Suzuki was, for an instant, ashamed for her.

" Occasionally that happens, too, I believe."

Every doubt had been resolved in her favor.

" An' if they got a nize bebby yaet – don' they – ah, don'*aeverybody*lig that?"

" I did, very much. Mine is a fine boy."

" Sa-ay/ He loog lig you – purple eye, bald hairs, pink cheek?"

" I 'm afraid he does."

"Traid?"

" Glad, then."

"Oh! 'Fraid mean glad? Yaes. Tha' 's way Mr. B. F. Pikkerton talking – *don*'mean what he say an' don' say what he mean – ezag'."

The consul laughed, but he could not quite understand the drift of her questioning.

" If people have a nize bebby alig that, they don' give him away, not to nob'y – nob'y – they don'*lig?*What you thing? "

" I should think not! " For a moment he looked savage as a young father can.

Cho-Cho-San's face glowed. She stood consciously aside, that the consul might the better see the baby on Suzuki's back. He understood, and smiled in the good-fellowship of newparenthood. He made some play with the child, and called him a fine fellow.

" Ah! You naever seen no soach bebby, I egspeg? "

In the largess of his fellowship he declared that he had not. He had only recently been engaged in putting the same question to his friends. She had hoped, indeed, that he would go on from that and say more, the subject so abundantly merited it; but she now remembered that, in her haste to satisfy her doubts, she had neglected all those innumerable little inquiries which go to make up the graceful game of Japanese courtesy. Though she might neglect them with Pinker- ton, she must not with a stranger who was obliging her.

SECTION 10

GENTLE LYING

"AH! How is that health? Also,2.I am sawry I woke you up, excellent, an' that I interrup' your languages. That is not a happy for the most exalted health – to be wake up an' interrup'. Therefore, I pray your honorable pardon. An' – how *is* that health?"

The consul said that he was quite well.

" Ah, *how* that is nize! An' you always sleeping well, most honorable?"

He nodded.

" Yaes – I hear you sleep. Oh! Tha' 's not joke! No, no, no! "

He had laughed, but she would never do that.

" But I do – snore, I believe – sometimes."

He was not proud of even this, of course.

"*Oh!* jus' lig gen-tie bree-zes."

He said that he could not do better than adopt this charming euphemism.

" Also, how ole you gitting ver' soon? "

" Thirty."

A Japanese always adds a few years. She therefore thought him younger, and her veneration abated accordingly. But he was in fact older.

" Tha' 's also nize – ver' nize. I

s'*is beauty'*
wish I so ole. That Mr. B. F. Pikker- ton he lig me more if I older, I thing." She
sighed.

"I don't know about that. The American point of view differs." But he would not
meddle. " How old are you, pray? "

This was only the proper return for her courtesy. Besides, the consul was enjoying
the usually dull game of decorum to-day. The girl was piquant in a most dazzling
fashion.

"Me? I 'bout – 'bout – " (what he had said made her doubt a little the Japanese
idea) " 'bout 'mos' twenty- seven when the chrysanthemum blooms again."

She was seventeen.

" Yaes, 'bout 'mos' – twenty-seven " – with a barely perceptible rising inflection.

He acquiesced in the fiction, but smiled at the way she hung her head and blushed;
this was not the Japanese way of telling one's age (or any other gentle lie).

" You got a grandmother? " she proceeded.

" Two," alleged the consul.

" Tha' *'s*ver' splen-did. An' is she well in her healths also?"

"Which one?"

She passed the joke, if she saw it. No Japanese will make his parent the subject of
one.

" The ole one – always the ole one firs'."

The consul felt queerly chidden.

" She was well at last accounts." "Tha"snize. An'the young one?" " The same.
And now, about yours?"

" Alas! I have not that same happiness lig you. I got not ancestors whichever. They
all angery account that Mr. B. F. Pikkerton, so they outcast me out the family. He
don' lig that they live with him, account they bag nombers. He an' me go'n' be only
bag nomber, he say. He big boss bag nomber, me jus' liddle boss bag nomber.*Me?*I
don' got ancestors before me nor behine me now. Hence they don' show me the way
to Meido when I die. Well, me? I don' keer whichever. I got hosban' an' bebby tha' 's
mos' bes' nize in Japan, mebbyin the whole worl'. An' I kin go at Nirvana by 'nother
road, aha! if I moast."

The kindly consul better than she understood both the effect of this separation
of her from her " ancestors," and the temperament of Pinkerton. He undertook,
notwithstanding his resolution not to meddle, a tentative remonstrance. She listened
politely, but he made no impression.

" You must not break with your relatives. If Pinkerton should not, should – well,
die, you know, you would indeed be an outcast. If your own people would have
nothing to do with you, nobody else would. It must, of course, be known to you that
your – marriage with Pinkerton has putyou in unfortunate relations with everybody;
the Japanese because you have offended them, the foreigners because he has. What
would you do in such a case? "

" Me? I could – dance, mebby, or

But she laughed as she said it. Then she acknowledged his rebuking glance.

"*Aexcuse*me, tha' 's not – nize? Well, it is not so easy to die as it was – bifore he came." She sighed happily.

The consul was curious.

"Why?" he asked.

"Why? – He make my life more sweet."

" But that is no reason for quarreling with your family."

"*But*they don' wan'*me,*because my hosban' don' wan'*them!*Henceforth I got go 'way from my hosban' if I wan' them; an' if I wan' him more bedder, I got go 'way from them. No madder whichever, I got go 'way from*some*one. Well, I wan' those hosban' more bedder than any. Sa-ay/ Tha' 's a foanny! They make me marry with him when / don' wish him; now I am marry with him,*they*don' wish him. Jus', after my father he kill his- self sticking with short sword, tha' 's how we gitting so poor – oh, ver' poor! Me? I go an' dance liddle, so we don' starve. Also, I thing if somebody wish me I git married for while, account that grandmother got have food an' clothings.*Well,*those ver' grandmother she as' the ole nakodo 'bout it; she lig me git marry with some one. He say mans jus' as' him other day kin he git him nize wife, an' he don' know none nizer."

She paused to let the consul make sure of this fact, which he did, and then acknowl- edged the appreciation she had provoked with a charming smile.

" Whichever, he say he thing I don' lig him, account he America-jin, he also remarking with me that he a barbarian an' a beas'.*Well,*me? – I say I don' wan' him. I 'fraid beas'.*But*aevery one else they say yaes – yaes, ah, yaes – he got*moaney,*an' for jus' liddle while I got endure him. So I say, 'Bring me that beas'.' An' lo!one day the ole nakodo he bringing him for look-at meeting.*Well!* – "

She paused to laugh, and so infectious was it that the consul adventurously joined her.

" At firs' I thing him a*god,*he so tall an' beautiful, and got on such a blue clothes all full golden things. An' he don' sit 'way, 'way off, an' jus' – *talk!*"

She laughed abandonedly.

" He make my life so ver' joyous, I thing I noever been that happy."

She had an access of demureness.

"Oh, jus' at firs' I frighten'; account he sit so*close*with me – an' hoi' my han' – an' as' if it made satin. Aha, ha, ha! Satin! Loog! "

She gave them both to him. They*"Pitiful Kivannnn"*

were deliciously pretty; but the consul was embarrassed by his possession of them. She began slowly to withdraw them, and then he let them go with regret.

" I beg your august pardon. I jus' thinging in the inside me, an' speaking with the outside. Tha' 's not nize. You don' keer nothing – 'bout – that – those?"

"What?"

He thought she meant the hands – and perhaps she did.

" Jus' those – liddle – story."

"Yes, I do," declared the consul, with some relief; "it is a charming story." And it was, for Cho-Cho- San's eyes and hands took part in its telling as well as her lips.

" You mean – you lig hear more? "

" Yes."

She reflected an instant.

" I thing there is no more. Jus' – yaes, jus' after while I naever git frighten' no more – no madder how close, nor how he hoi' my hand."

" But then you – I beg pardon – you were married? I think you said so? "

" Oh, yaes," she replied, as if that had made little difference in their situation; " I marry with him."

" I think his ship was then ordered to – "

She nodded.

" Alas! he got go an' serve his country. But he go'n' come back, an' keep on being marry with me. What you thing? "

The consul contrived to evade the interrogation.

" Is that why you asked about the robins?"

" Yaes; he go'n' come when the robins nest again.*He?*He don' naever egspeg we got this nize bebby, account I don' tell him. I don' kin tell him. I don' know where he is. But – *me?*I don' tell if I know, account he rush right over here, an' desert his country, an' henceforth git in a large trouble – mebby with that President United States America, an' that large Goddess Liberty Independence! What you thing? " XI

" THE MOS' BES' NIZE MAN "

IT was quite superfluous to point out such of her ideas as had birth in the fertile brain of Pinkerton. Certainly he had enjoyed his married life with her, but it was for another reason than hers. The consul could observe, he thought, how exquisitely amusing it had been. It was, too, exactly in Pinkerton's line to take this dainty, vivid, eager, formless material, and mold it to his most wantonly whimsical wish. It was perhaps fortunate for her that his country had had need of him so soon after his marriage.

However, the consul informed her that her fears of trouble for Pinkerton from the sources mentioned were entirely groundless. But this, to his surprise, was not pleasing intelligence. She liked to believe (as he had let her believe) that Pinkerton occupied a large space in the affairs of his country; that he was under the special patronage of the President, and the Goddess of Liberty was, perhaps, her own corollary. But it fitted his character as she had conceived it. To her he was a god, perhaps. But let it be understood that a Japanese god is neither austere nor immaculate.

" Well, whichever," she said, in some disappointment, " tha' 's a so'- prise on him when he come. He alltimes joking with me; I make one joke upon him. Tha' 's good joke. What you thing? "

The consul shook his head. The matter began to have a sinister look. But the girl's faith was sublime.

"Ah-h-h!*You?*"Her inflection was one of pity for his ignorance. " Tha' 's account you don' know him, you shaking your nize head. He joking all times. Sometime I dunno*if*he joking, aercep' he stop, look solemn, an' laugh.*Then*he make the house raddle! Oh, mebby you thing I don' joke too, also? Well, tha' 's mw-take. I make joke jus' lig him – jus' bad. One time I make joke with him 'bout run 'way to that grandmother, account I don' keer for him no more.

Well – what you thing? He say, ' 'Ello! Less see how you kin run fas'.' Aha, ha, ha! Tha' 's liddle joke upon me. Now I go'n' have the larges' joke upon him. Sa-oy – you got tell him, if you please, augustness, that I could n't wait, it was so long – long

– long! I got tire'. So – I am marry with a great an' wise prince name' Yama- dori Okyo, an' live in a huge castle with one thousan' servants, an' – an' all my hearts kin wish! Aha, ha, ha! Also, that I go'n' away to his castle with his purple-eye' bebby, to naever return no more – naever. You go'n' tell him that?"

" I would prefer not to have a hand in any further – that is, any deception," the consul objected gravely.

The girl was amazed and reproachful.

"Ah-h-h! Don' you lig joke? I thing aevery American do. Tha' 's not nize for me. I got be sawry I telling you all those. Alas!*How*that would be nize for you! You see him git angery so quick." She smote her hands together. " An' then he say those remark 'bout debbil an' hell, an' rush up the hill this away."

She again lifted her kimono, and acted it recklessly across the apartment.

" But, my dear madame – "

She came at him with a voice and movement that were resistlessly caressing. He perceived how useless it would be to protest further. He acknowledged her protean fascination.

"Lig those new porcelains of Kirtkosan"

" Ah-h-h!*Please,*augustness, to tell him? It will be that*nize*for me! Ah, you go'n' do it? – *Yaesf*Say so! "

The consul had capitulated to her voice and eyes. This was evident to her.

" Ah – thangs, most excellent. You the mos' bes' nize man in the worl' – "

She paused guiltily; even this purely Japanese euphemism might be conjugal treason.

" Except? " laughed the consul.

*"Aexcep'"*confessed the girl, with drooping head.

A smile began to grow upon her lips; when she raised her face it was a splendid laugh.

"*How*we have fun seeing him rush up that hill at the house " – she was frankly dissembling – " so! " She illustrated again – back and forth across the apartment. " After that – ah – after that – *well* – I make aevery- thing correc'."

She was radiantly certain that she could.

The consul remembered the saying of the professor of rhetoric that no comedy could succeed without its element of tragedy. Well, Pinkerton*might*have meant to return to her. Any other man probably would. He would not have been quite certain of himself. Only, that stuff about the robins sounded like one of his infernal jokes. He probably supposed that she knew what he meant – farewell; but she had not so construed it. Unless Pinkerton had changed, he had probably not thought of her again – except as the prompt wife of another man. He never explained anything. It was his theory that circumstances always did this for one; it was therefore a saving of energy to permit circumstances to do it. There was a saying in the navy that if any one could forget a played game or a spent bottle more quickly than Pinkerton, he had not yet been born. Providing her with a house and money meant nothing. He would probably have given her all he had, whether it were a dollar or a thousand. But, on the other hand, if she had been one of the sudden and insane fancies which occasionally visited him, the case was altogether different, and altogether like Pinkerton; for in the person of a fascinating woman the emotion might survive the absence in question. For himself, he was quite sure – had he been Pinker- ton, of course – that it would have survived something greater. And finally his own views prevailed with him as if they were Pinkerton's, and he believed that he would be delighted to return and resume his charming life with her on Higashi Hill.

He thereupon told her that Lieutenant Pinkerton's ship was under orders to stop at Nagasaki, the government rendezvous for the navy, about the first of September, to observe and report the probabilities of war with China; and he was instantly glad that he had told her.

The girl's superb joy was expressed in a long, indrawn sigh, and then silence.

But something had to be said – or done.

" I – I lig as' you 'nother thing – " again dissembling, as if the talk were still at the trivialities where it began.

" Certainly," said the consul, with a smile. " But won't you have a chair?"

He had noticed that she was trembling. She sat up unsteadily on the edge of it. And then she forgot what she meant to ask!

" Sa-oy/ – " She was still at sea. But suddenly a thought flashed in her eyes. " All bebbies at your America got those purple eye? "

" A – yes, very many of them," said the consul, with a little surprise at her direction.

"An – an' also bald of their head? "

" All of them, I believe, at first."

He smiled, and the girl smiled back at him engagingly.

"*Sa-ay,*augustness, he go'n' come for see those bebby? What you thing?" Her words were like caresses.

But the rapture growing surely in the girl's face now was not reflected in that of the consul. Concern for her outweighed her fascinations for the moment.

" I – I hope so – "

She cut off his doubting incontinently.

"*Sa-ay!*Mebby you also don' thing he go'n' take us live in his large castle at United States America? " she challenged reproachfully.

" Did he tell you that he would – that he had one?"

" No; he don' tell me – *nawthing.*He laugh, when I as' him, lig the house go'n' fall down.*But* – what you thing?"

The consul answered her quite briefly. He knew that he hurt her, but his impotent anger was at Pinkerton; he had not thought him capable of that.

" If I were to advise, I should ask you to consider seriously Yamadori's proposal, if he has really offered himself. It is a great and unusual opportunity for you – for any girl – in – in Japan."

" You – thing – those – ?*You? *"

She looked at him for an amazed and reproachful instant; then gathered her kimono in her hand, and pushed her feet into her clogs.

"Go before, Suzuki,"she said gently to the maid; to'the consul, sorrowfully, " Goon night."

At the door she turned with a ceremonial sweep of her draperies, looked, and came hurrying back. All the joy had returned to her face at the sincere regret – almost pain – she saw upon his. She impulsively grasped his hands – both of them.

" Once more – different – goon night, augustness." And her voice
They hid behind the shuji
was very soft. "Aha, ha, ha!*Me?*I jus' a foo-el – *yaes. You?* – you the mos' bes' nize man in all the whole worl' – "

She paused – smiling up at him. He understood that she wished to repeat their pretty play upon the phrase.

"Except?"

She nodded and laughed.

"Aexcsp' – Ha, ha, ha!"

She hurried after the maid, laughing back at him confessingly as she went.

And, after all, the consul was glad it had ended thus. For joy is better than sorrow – always and everywhere.

Whenthey again reached the pretty house on the hill, Cho-Cho-San lookedruefully back over the steep road they had come.

" Oh,*how*that was tiresome, Suzuki! But*the* – when he comes, it will be jus' – one – two – three great strides!*How*he will rush up that hill it cost us so much sweat to climb! Lig storm with lightening and thunder! Flash! flash! flash! Bourn! bourn! bourn! An' here he is – all for jus' liddle me! Then*how*he will stamp about – not removing his boots – spoiling the mats – smashing the fusuma – shaking the house lig earthquake animal! ' Where is she? Hah! Mans tole me she gone an' marry with a fool Yamadori! Gone me my purple- eye' bebby away.' Then I jump roun' his neck bifore he gitting*too*angery, an' hole his han', an' say, close with his ears: ' How do, Mr. B. F. Pikker- ton? ' Aha, ha, ha! What you thing, Suzuki?"

And Suzuki said, in English, too: " Tha' 's mos' bes' nize thing *I*a*ever*see!" XII
LIKE A PICTURE OF BUNCHOSAI

FROM that time until the seventeenth of September not a ship entered the harbor but under the scrutiny of the glass that Lieutenant Pin- kerton had left at the little house on Higashi Hill to read his signals aboard. And there were very many of them, for the war was imminent. Faith had begun to strain a little with unfaith, after the first. It was very long; but on the seventeenth his ship came into the bay. So like a great bird did she come that the glass didnot find her until her white-and-gold mass veered to make an anchorage. Then, all at once, the gilt name on her bow was before Cho-Cho-San's eyes. It was tragically sudden. With a hurtling cry, she fell to the floor. The little maid, with Eastern intuition, understood; but she said nothing, and did – what was best. Both she and her mistress – and all the world, for that matter – knew the comfort of this speechless, sympathetic service. And presently she was better, and could talk.

" I – I di'n' know I*so* – glad," softly laughed Cho-Cho-San.

But the maid had known what to expect.

" You go'n' res' liddle now, please, Oku-San! You go'n' sleep liddle – please, jus' liddle – res' ' – sleep?"

She drew her mistress's eyelids down, and lightly held them. Cho- Cho-San shook her off, and sprang up, revivified.

" Res'! Sleep! Not till he come! "

" Res' – peace – sleep – *beauty,"* chanted the maid, persuasively. But her mistress would not.

" Now, hasten lig you got eagle's wings an' a thousan' feet! It will not be one hour – not one half – till he will be here. My pink kimono – widest obi – kanzashi for my hair – an' poppies. I will be more beautiful than I have aever been. Flowers – alas! there are no cherry-blossoms. *How* that is sad! Seem lig we cannot be gay without them. In the month of the cherry-blossoms we were marry! But chrysanthemums – all of them! An' lanterns if it be black night – 'mos' one thousan'! Aha, ha, ha! His house shall be gayer than it has aever been. There shall naever again be such good occasion."

" Res' is beauty," urged the maid, holding up the mirror to her.

" Ah, Suzuki! I *am* beautiful – as beautiful as when he went away? "

The maid was silent – the Japanese silence which is *not* assent.

Cho-Cho-San snatched the metallic mirror out of her hand.

" I *am!"* she cried. "Say so!"

She brandished the heavy mirror over the girl's head.

"I as' you to res' – peace – sleep. Tha' 's way git beautiful once more."

"Oh-h-h! 'Once more'!" The mirror crashed to the floor, and she burst into tears.

" Jus' – you been too trouble'. Now you go'n' res' liddle," urged the comforting maid.

"Oh, all the gods! I cannot! – I cannot till he come. I shall die bifore."

She sorrowfully recovered the mirror.

" No – no; pitiful Kwannon, I am no longer beautiful! Waiting an' doubting make one soon sad an' old. An' how long we have wait! – how long! Oh, Shaka! But now I am happy – happier than I have aever been. Therefore shall I be more beautiful than I have aever been again. For happiness also is beauty. Ah, Suzuki, be kine with me!" She got on her knees to the maid, and laid her head at her feet. An ecstatic thought came to her. " Suzuki, *you* shall make me beautiful to-day, an' to-morrow the gods shall. Now we have not even time to pray them – not time to res'. Will you not? Can you not? Ah-h-h! You *moast!"*

She pulled the girl down to her, and whispered the last words in her ear – with her arms about her.

And the girl did. Let us not inquire how. She had never yet withstood that tone and that caress. There was a certain magic in her deft fingers, and her mistress had it all. No daintier creature need one ever wish to see than this bride awaiting anew the coming of her husband.

And when it was all done, they each took a final delighted look into the mirror. It was too small tq show the whole figure, but they moved it up and down and round about until every portion had been seen. They both pronounced it very good.

" Stan' jus' that way," begged the maid, going the length of the apartment to observe. " Jus' lig those new porcelains of Kinkozan!" she declared.

" Jus' lig those ole picture of Bun- chosai! " retorted Cho- Cho- San – meaning anything but that.

But – in the way of women the

She lighted the andon

world over – a few more touches were necessary – and *it* was finished.

" Now the flowers for his room! Take them all – oh, a every one! We shall not need them again. Go – go – *go!* Aha, ha, ha! An' Trouble- make a picture of him! He will be Trouble no longer after to-day. He go'n' git new name – mebby Joy! – Joy!"

Her commands were obeyed. Within the appointed hour the house was decked as for a festival, and not a flower remained upon its stem. The baby had indeed become a picture; and so had Cho-Cho-San and the maid and the house.

Then they hid behind the shoji, recklessly making peep-holes with their dampened fingers, as they had planned. There was one very low down for the baby, so that he could sit on the mats, – which he did not choose to do, – and one each for the others.

Cho-Cho-San sang as she fixed herself at her peep-hole – so as not to disarrange her finery:

" Rog-a-by, bebby, off in Japan,
You jus' a picture off of a fan."

The maid tossed the baby like a ball into her lap.

" Aha, ha, ha!" laughed Madame Butterfly once more.

Everything was at last quite as they had planned it.

" Now let him come," she said, in a charming defiance – " let him come – quickly – an' – then – "

The hour passed. Then two – four. Night fell. They ceased to chatter. Later came perfect silence; then that other silence of the dead of the night. The pulses of terror quickened. Suzuki noiselessly lighted the lanterns. Later, at a shivering gesture from her mistress, she lighted the andon in their room; then the hibachi. She had grown very cold. All night they watched. He had the careless habit of the night. But he did not come.

And all the next day they watched, and many after, quite silent now, always. The baby wondered at this, and would look inquiringly from one to the other. It was very strange to him, this new silence. The house had been full always of their laughter and chatter – the patter of their feet – the sighing of the shoji. They did nothing now but watch – and eat a little, sleep a little – less and less of these. Finally Cho-Cho-San could no longer hold the glass. She lay on the mats with the baby, while the faithful handmaid watched. Every day the faded flowers were replaced by purchased ones – cheaper and cheaper ones. Their last money went for this and the candles which renewed the lights of the lanterns each night. These were not a thousand – were not a dozen – now.

She did not think of going to him. In destroying her Japanese conventions this was the one thing that had been left. In " Onna Yushoku Mibea Bunko" ("The Young Ladies' Old Book of Decorum ") she had read that the only woman who seeks a male is a yujo, a courtezan.

In a week a passenger-steamer came into the bay. They took no interest in her. But the next day, quite by accident, they saw him for the first time. He was on the deck of the strange ship. A blonde woman was on his arm. They watched quite sleeplessly all that night. A few more lanterns were lighted.

On the following morning the warship had disappeared from the harbor.

Cho-Cho-San was frightened. The sinking at her heart she now knew tobe black doubt. Her little, unused, frivolous mind had not forecast such a catastrophe. There might have been a reason, she had conceived, for his detention aboard his ship. He was never very certain. She had not been sure that he was with her until the day before; the position of the vessel had been unfavorable for observation.

11

SECTION 11

XIII

THE GOOD CONSUL'S COMPASSIONATE LYING

DEMORALIZATION set in. Even the comfort of the maid was dulled. They decided that Cho-Cho- San should go to see the good consul, while the maid and the baby remained at home to welcome him if, perhaps, he had not gone with the war-ship. They had already created this hope.

The maid helped her down the steepest part of the hill. Nevertheless, when she arrived at the consulate she was quite breathless. The consul was alone. There were no frivolities now. Each knew that the other understood.

"Me? I got – liddle heart-illness, I thing," the girl panted in excuse of her lack of ceremony and the consul's pitying stare. She looked very ill; but her smile was still tragically bright.

The consul placed her a chair. She declined it. There was a moment of conscious silence. Then he went hesitatingly to his desk, and got an envelop containing money – a large sum. He silently handed her this.

She looked at him in appealing inquiry, but she did not take the money.

" It is only – only in remembrance of the – the past. He wishes you to be always happy – as – he says he is. He confidently hopes for your good wishes and congratulations."

The maid knelt to take off her shoes

There was moisture in the consul's eyes, only questioning in hers. He suddenly saw that she did not understand. He decided that she never should. He did not speak again, nor did she for a space. Then:

"Happy – happy?" she murmured dizzily. *"But* – how kin *I* be happy if he do not come? How kin *he* be – happy – if – he do not come? "

The consul was silent. He still held the money toward her. She tried to smile a little, to make him think she was indifferent concerning his answer to the question she was about to ask.

" Ah – oh – *ah!* You tole him 'bout – 'bout that joke – that liddle joke we make on him? "

The consul pretended ignorance. She explained:

" That 'bout me go'n' marry with Yamadori, an' take his bebby 'way? "

He had to answer now:

" Oh, that was – too – too foolish to talk about seriously."

Pinkerton had been glad to hear it.

" But – you – *tole* him? "

She hoped now he had not.

" Well – "

He looked out of the window. He would not strike, but she would be struck.

" But – you – you *tole* him? " She had raised her voice piteously.

" Yes," answered the consul, dully, wondering what he could say next.

She gasped, and wiped her dry lips.

"Yaes; tha' 's – right. Tha' 's – what I – as' you do. An' – an' what he – *say?* "she questioned huskily.

The consul was willing to lie as deeply as the occasion might demand. The woe in the girl's face afflicted him. He saw in her attire the pitiful preparations to welcome the husband he now knew to be a craven, and in her face what it had cost to wait for him. But in specie the lie was difficult.

" Well," he began uncertainly, " we – it all happened about as you had supposed. He got very angry, and would have rushed right up the hill, as you thought, only – only – " What next? The wish to lie had grown upon him wondrously as he went on. But invention flagged. The despatches on his desk caught his eye. " Only – he was not permitted a moment's leave while in the harbor. He had all these despatches to prepare – for – for his government – the war, you know. All in cipher."

He showed them to her. A brilliant thought came into his head.

" See! They are all in his handwriting."

He had not written a line of them.

" His ship was ordered away suddenly to China; but he '11 be back here some of these fine days, and then – "

The rest was for her. At any rate, he could lie no more.

" All – all the gods in heaven bless – you," she said, sinking with the reaction.

She reeled, and he put her into thechair. Her head fell limply back, and her pallid face looked up at him with the weary eyes closed. But there was rest and peace on it, and it was still very beautiful.

Some one was approaching in haste,, and he drew a screen before her.

12

SECTION 12

XIV

THE BLONDE WOMAN

A WOMAN entered. " Mr. Sharpless – the American consul? " she asked, while crossing the threshold.

The consul bowed. " Can you reach my husband at Kobe – by telegraph? "

" I think so. Who is your husband?"

He took up a writing-pad as he spoke.

" Lieutenant Pinkerton of the – "

" One moment, for God's sake! "

It was too late. The eyes of the little woman in the chair were fixed on his. They even tried to smile a little, wearily, at the poor result of his compassionate lying. She shook her head for silence.

"I beg your pardon; I 'm – I am – ready – " said the consul, roughly. He made no other explanation. " Proceed."

" I should like you to send this telegram: ' Just saw the baby and his nurse. Can't we have him at once? He is lovely. Shall see the mother about it to-morrow. Was not at home when I was there to-day. Expect to join you Wednesday week per*Kioto Maru.*May I bring him along?

'Adelaide.'"

As she advanced and saw Cho-Cho- San, she stopped in open admiration.

" How very charming – how*lovely* – you are, dear! Will you kiss me, you pretty – *plaything!* "

Cho-Cho-San stared at her with round eyes – as children do when afraid. Then her nostrils quivered and her lids slowly closed.

" No," she said, very softly.

" Ah, well," laughed the other, " I don't blame you. They say you don't do that sort of thing – to women, at any rate. I quite forgive our men for falling in love with you. Thanks for permitting me to interrupt you. And, Mr. Sharpless, will you get that off at once? Good day!"

She went with the hurry in which

"J<areiL>ell, liddle maiden"

she had come. It was the blonde woman they had seen on the deck of the passenger-steamer.

They were quite silent after she was gone – the consul still at his desk, his head bowed impotently in his hands.

Cho-Cho-San rose presently, and staggered toward him. She tried desperately to smile, but her lips were tightly drawn against her teeth. Searching unsteadily in her sleeve, she drew out a few small coins, and held them out to him. He curiously took them on his palm.

" They are his, all that is left of his beautiful moaney. I shall need no more. Give them to him. I lig if you also say I sawry – no, no,*no!*glad – glad – *glad!"*She humbly sighed."*Me?*I – I wish him that happiness same lig he wish for himself – an' – an* – me.*Me?*I shall – be happy – mebby. Tell him I – shall be – happy."

Her head drooped for a moment. When she raised it she was quite emotionless, if one might judge from her face.

" Thang him – that Mr. B. F. Pik- kerton – also for all that kineness he have been unto me. Permit me to thang*you,*augustness, for that same. You – you " – she could smile a little now at the pretty recollection – then the tears came slowly into her eyes – " you – the mos' bes' nize man – in all the – whole – worl'."

She closed her eyes a moment, and stood quite still.

The consul said below his breath:

" Pinkerton, and all such as

he!"

" Goon night," said Cho-Cho-San, and at the door looking back, " Sayo- nara," and another tired smile.

She staggered a little as she went out.

"Alas, you also have seen her!" wailed the intuitive little maid, as she let her mistress in.

" An' she is more beautiful than the Sun-Goddess," answered Cho-Cho- San.

The maid knelt to take off her shoes.

" She – she thing me – jus' a – plaything."

She generously tried to smile at the maid, who was weeping. She touched her hair caressingly as she knelt.

" Don' weep for me, liddle maiden – account I disappoint – a liddle – disappoint – Don' weep for me. That liddle while ago you as' me to res' – peace – sleep," she said after a while, wearily. " Well, go 'way, an' I will – res'. Now I*wish*to res' – sleep. Long – long sleep. An' I pray you, loog, when you see me again, whether I be not again beautiful – again as a bride."

The maid did not go. Once more she understood her mistress.

"But – I thing*you*loave me? "

The girl sobbed.

" Therefore go – that I suffer nomore. Go, that I res' – peace – sleep. Long – beautiful sleep! Go, I beg."

She gently took her hands and led her out.

" Farewell, liddle maiden," she said softly, closing the shoji. " Don' weep." XV

WHEN THE ROBINS NEST AGAIN

SHE sat quite still, and waited till night fell. Then she lighted the andon, and drew her toilet-glass toward her. She had a sword in her lap as she sat down. It was the one thing of her father's which her relatives had permitted her to keep. It would have been very beautiful to a Japanese, to whom the sword is a soul. A golden dragon writhed about the superb scabbard. He had eyes erf rubies, and held in his mouth a sphere of crystal which meant many mystical things to a Japanese. The guard wasa coiled serpent of exquisite workmanship. The blade was tempered into vague shapes of beasts at the edge. It was signed, " Ikesada." To her father it had been Honor. On the blade was this inscription:

To die with Honor When one can no longer live with Honor.

It was in obscure ideographs; but it was also written on her father's kaimyo at the shrine, and she knew it well.

" To die with honor – " She drew the blade affectionately across her palm. Then she made herself pretty with vermilion and powder and perfumes; and she prayed, humbly endeavoring at the last to make her peace. She had not forgotten the mission-ary'sreligion; but on the dark road from death to Meido it seemed best noV to trust herself to the compassionate au- gustnesses, who had always been true. Then she placed the point of the weapon at that nearly nerveless spot in the neck known to every Japanese, and began to press it slowly inward. She could not help a little gasp at the first incision. But presently she could feel the blood finding its way down her neck. It divided on her shoulder, the larger stream going down her bosom. In a moment she could see it making its way daintily between her breasts. It began to congeal there. She pressed on the sword, and a fresh stream swiftly overran the other – redder, she thought. And then suddenly she could

She had a sword in her lap as she sat down

no longer see it. She drew the mirror closer. Her hand was heavy, and the mirror seemed far away. She knew that she must hasten. But even as she locked her fingers on the serpent of the guard, something within her cried out piteously. They had taught her how to die, but he had taught her how to live – nay, to make life sweet. Yet that was the reason she must die. Strange reason! She now first knew that it was sad to die. He had come, and substituted himself for everything; he had gone, and left her nothing – nothing but this.

Themaid softly put the baby into the room. She pinched him, and he began to cry.

"Oh, pitiful Kwannon! Nothing?"

The sword fell dully to the floor. The stream between her breasts darkened and stopped. Her head drooped slowly forward. Her arms penitently outstretched themselves toward the shrine. She wept.

"Oh, pitiful Kwannon!" she prayed.

The baby crept cooing into her lap. The little maid came in and bound up the wound.

WhenMrs. Pinkerton called next day at the little house on Higashi Hill it was quite empty.

CPSIA information can be obtained at www.ICGtesting.com
Printed in the USA
LVOW041649291111

257016LV00001B/131/P

9 781151 718181